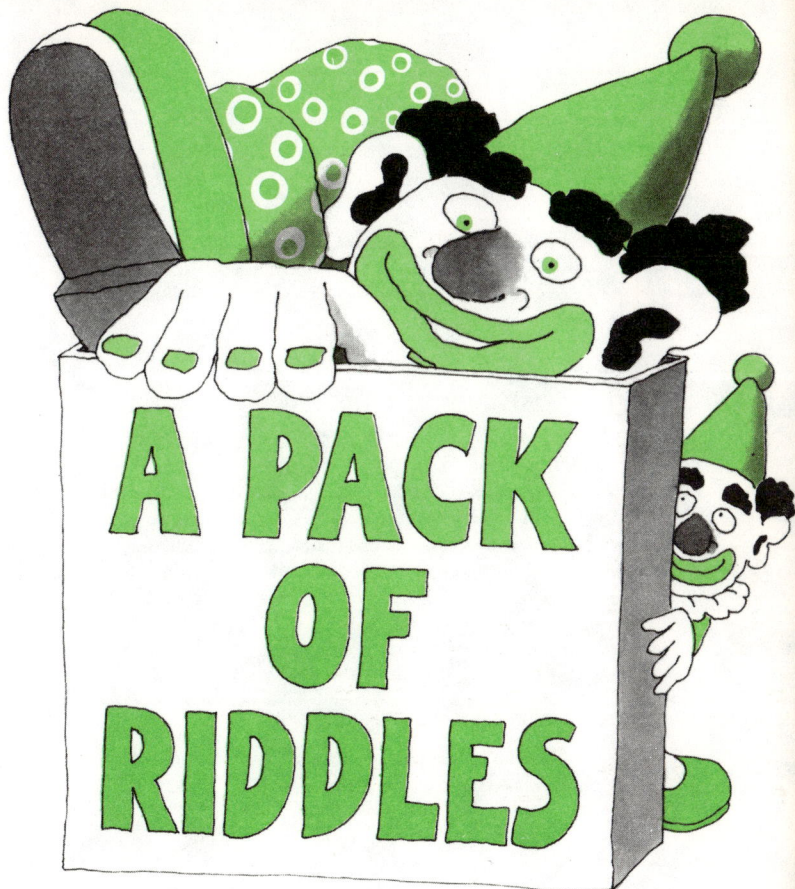

A PACK OF RIDDLES

compiled by
William R. Gerler

illustrated by
Giulio Maestro

STARSTREAM PRODUCTS
WINSTON-SALEM, NORTH CAROLINA

STARSTREAM PRODUCTS EDITION

This edition published by arrangement with E.P. Dutton & Co., Inc.,
New York.

Library of Congress Cataloging in Publication Data

Gerler, William R.   A pack of riddles

SUMMARY: A collection of riddles such as "What color
is a hiccup?" and "Why are fish so smart?"

1. Riddles—Juvenile literature.   [1. Riddles]
I. Maestro, Giulio.   II. Title.

1 2 3 4 5 6 7 8 9 10   December 1980

Designed by Giulio Maestro
Printed in the U.S.A.

Starstream Products
P.O. Box 2222
Winston-Salem, N.C. 27102

To Kristine and Robyn Sorensen,
my two granddaughters, who will
enjoy this book for many years

What kind of animals can jump higher than a house?

All kinds of animals. A house can't jump.

What did the leopard say when he was done with dinner?

Mmmm, that hit the spot, the spot, the spot.

What happens when you give a cat
lemonade?

You get a sour puss.

Why is it cheap to feed a giraffe?

Because he makes a little food go a long way.

What do you get when you cross an owl with a goat?

A hootenanny.

What do you get when you cross a cocker spaniel, a poodle, and a rooster?

A cockerpoodledoo.

Why is an elephant so wrinkled?

Because you can't iron him.

Dog Owner: Come now, Rover, speak!
Speak! Speak!

Dog: What shall I say?

Why does a hummingbird hum?

Because he doesn't know the words.

What kind of bird is like a car?

A goose. They both honk.

Did you hear about the two kangaroos
that jumped into each other's pockets
and were never seen again?

What quacks louder than a duck?

Two ducks.

What's a raisin?

A grape that worries too much.

Why are Boy Scouts so tired on the first day of April?

Because they've just had a thirty-one-day March.

Why can't you milk a mouse?

Because a pail won't fit under it.

What animal likes Leap Year?

The kangaroo.

What man's business is best when things are the dullest?

A knife sharpener's.

What did one lightning bug say to the other?

Give me a push. I think my battery is dead.

What is a sleeping bull called?

A bull-dozer.

Doctor: What seems to be your trouble?

Patient: I think I'm a dog.

Doctor: How long has this been going on?

Patient: Oh, ever since I was a puppy.

How did Mr. and Mrs. Octopus come
aboard the Ark?

Arm in arm, in arm, in arm.

Alvin was viewing a cage of green parakeets in a pet-shop window.

"Look, Mother, there are some canaries that aren't ripe yet."

Have you ever seen a fish cry?

No, but I've seen a whale blubber.

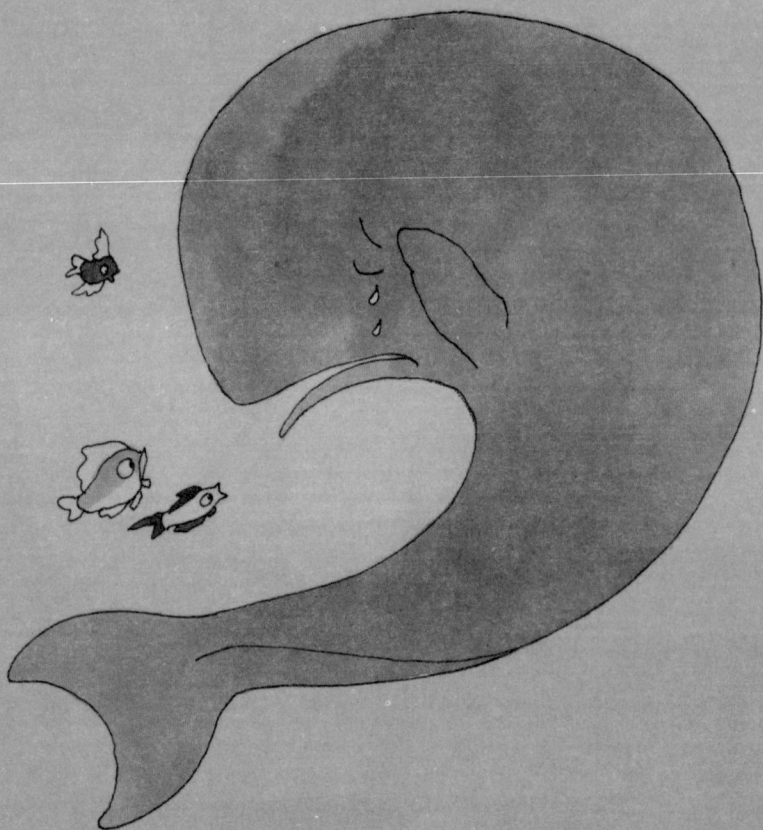

What kind of fish is good on toast
in the morning?

Jelly-fish.

What is green, noisy, and extremely dangerous?

A stampeding herd of pickles.

What's green and has whiskers?

A lime that needs a shave.

What is the best thing to put into a pie?

Your teeth.

Why is baking a cake like a baseball game?

They both depend on the batter.

What do you get if you cross a
potato plant with an onion?

Potatoes with watery eyes.

What is a volcano?

A mountain with hiccups.

What color is a hiccup?

Burple.

What has three feet but can't stand?

A yardstick.

Who carries a trunk without a handle?

An elephant.

What animals need to be oiled?

Mice, because they squeak.

Why do birds fly south?

Because it's too far to walk.

Did you hear about the dog who went
to a flea circus and stole the show?

What was the matter with the little house that was sick?

It had a window-pane (pain).

What has a hundred teeth but no
mouth?

A saw.

Why did the centipede wear galoshes?

Because his sneakers were in the wash.

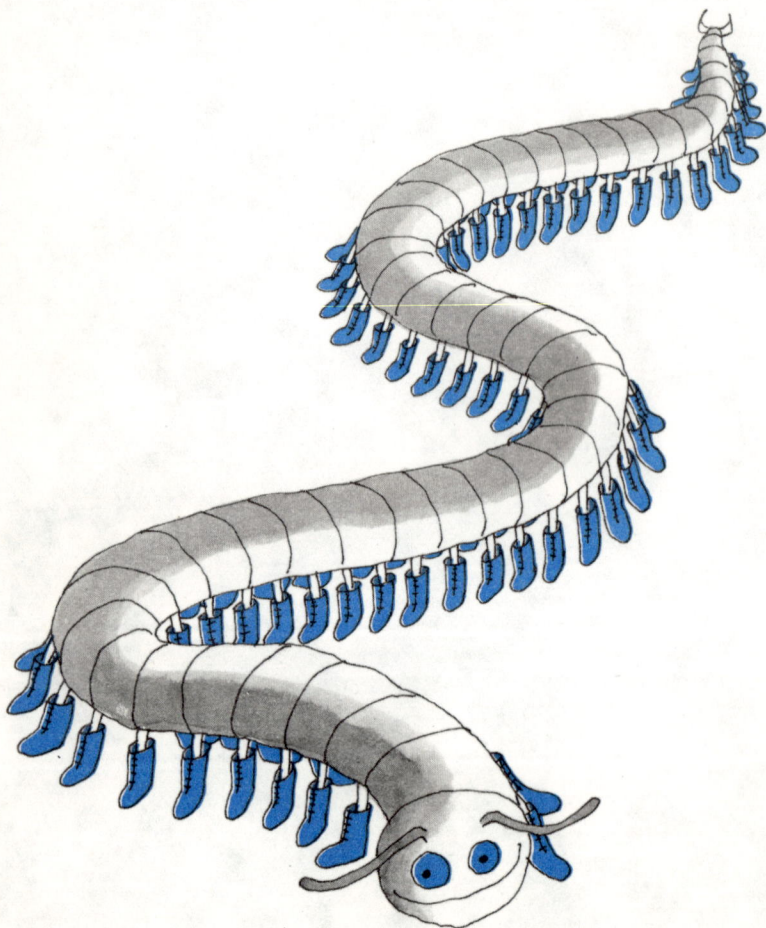

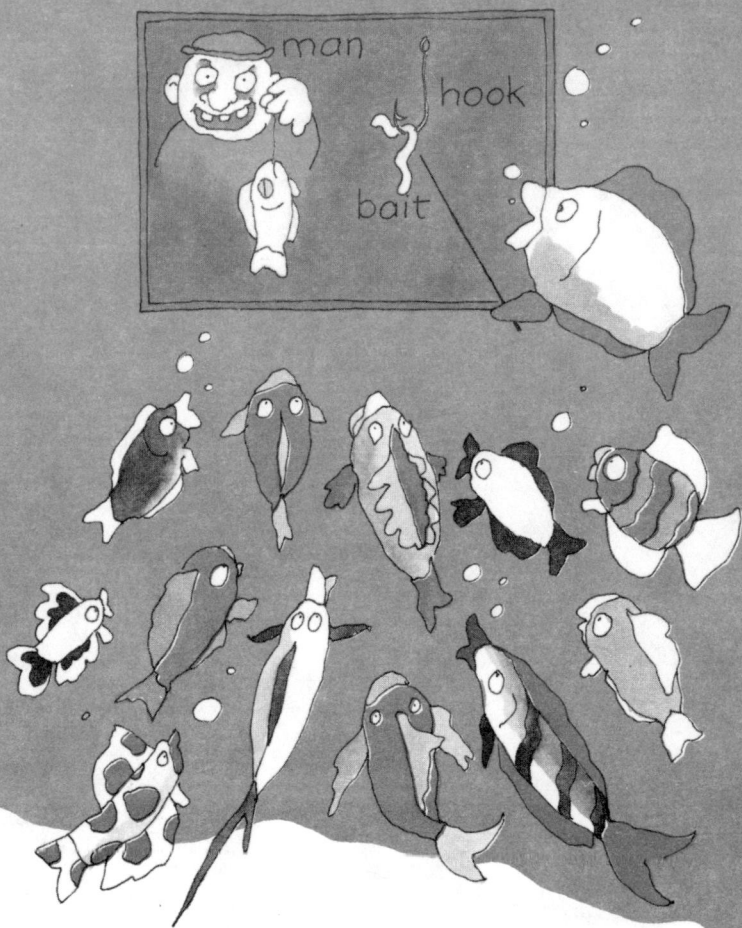

Why are fish so smart?

They always go around in schools.

What comes up to the door but never gets in?

The steps.

What kind of room has no doors, no windows, and no walls?

A mush-room.

Why should you cut a hole in your umbrella?

So you can see when it stops raining.

Where do vampires get their mail?

At the ghost office.

What is the only nail a carpenter
hates to hit?

His fingernail.

What flowers do cooks use?

Butter-cups.

What can speak all the languages of the world?

An echo.

Why isn't your nose twelve inches
long?

Because, if it were, it would be
a foot.

What kind of paper makes the best
kites?

Fly paper.

Why is an empty purse always the same?

Because you can't see any change in it.

Why is it hard to talk with a goat around?

He keeps butting in.

What can you serve but not eat?

A tennis ball.

What is the difference between an old penny and a shiny dime?

Nine cents.

If all the cars in this nation were pink, what would we have?

A pink-car-nation.

What can you hold in your left hand but not in your right hand?

Your right elbow.

What has a head and a tail but no body?

A coin.

Why is it useless to send a letter to Washington today?

Because he died in 1799.

Who invented the first airplane that didn't fly?

The Wrong Brothers.

What is the quietest game in the world?

Bowling. You can hear a pin drop.

What did the beach say to the ocean?

Hi, tide.

What can give you power to see
through brick walls?

Windows.

What's green and yellow and seldom rings?

An unlisted banana.

What kind of beans will never grow in a garden?

Jelly beans.

Teacher: Will someone tell me where the English Channel is?

Student: I don't know. We can't get it on our set.

Why is tennis such a noisy game?

Because each player raises a racket.

Son: Dad, what is the cleanest race in the world?

Dad: The soapbox derby.

What kind of keys won't open doors?

Monkeys, turkeys, and donkeys.

What did the digital clock say to
its mother?

Look, Ma, no hands.

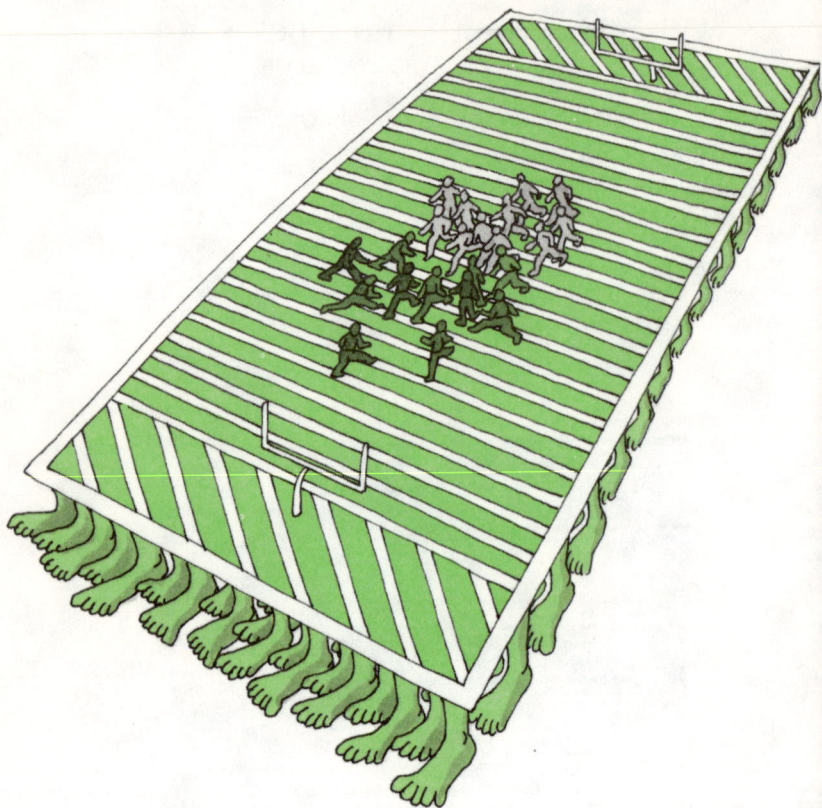

What has three hundred feet, is green with stripes, and stepped on by people?

A football field.

What did one math book say to the other?

I've got problems.

What gets up in the morning and waves all day?

The flag.

What did one octopus say to another?

I want to hold your hand, hand, hand, hand.

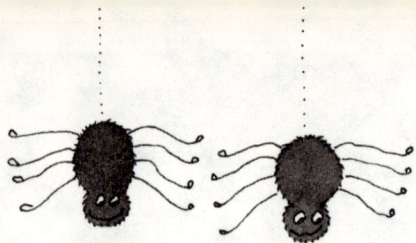

What animals didn't come to the Ark in pairs (pears)?

Worms. They came in apples.

Why is a barn so noisy?

Because the cows have horns.

WILLIAM R. GERLER is a public relations executive whose books for adults have included collections of humor. He is a graduate of the University of Illinois and lives in Racine, Wisconsin.

GIULIO MAESTRO is a versatile illustrator and graphic designer. Recent books include the Dutton title *Egg-ventures* by Harry Milgrom, *Three Kittens* by Mirra Ginsburg, and *Who Said Meow?* by Maria Polushkin (both Crown). He lives in Madison, Connecticut.

The title is hand-lettered and the display and text type are set in Janson Alphatype. The art is line and wash with overlays of an alternating second color.